J TRIPP
Tripp, Valerie, 1951-
Kit saves the day

# The American Girls

17  74

FELICITY, a spunky, spritely colonial girl,
full of energy and independence

18  24

JOSEFINA, an Hispanic girl whose heart and
hopes are as big as the New Mexico sky

18  54

KIRSTEN, a pioneer girl of strength and
spirit who settles on the frontier

18  64

ADDY, a courageous girl determined to be
free in the midst of the Civil War

19  04

SAMANTHA, a bright Victorian beauty, an
orphan raised by her wealthy grandmother

19  34

KIT, a clever, resourceful girl facing the
Great Depression with spirit and determination

19  44

MOLLY, who schemes and dreams on the
home front during World War Two

1934

# KIT
# SAVES
# THE DAY
## *A Summer Story*

By VALERIE TRIPP

ILLUSTRATIONS  WALTER RANE

VIGNETTES  SUSAN McALILEY

American Girl

Published by Pleasant Company Publications
For information, address: Book Editor, Pleasant Company Publications,
8400 Fairway Place, P.O. Box 620998, Middleton, WI 53562.

Printed in the United States of America.
01 02 03 04 05 06 07 08 QWT 12 11 10 9 8 7 6 5 4 3 2 1

PICTURE CREDITS
The following individuals and organizations have generously given
permission to reprint images contained in "Looking Back":
pp. 64-65—Library of Congress, photo by Dorothea Lange (family on the road);
© Bettmann/CORBIS (sitting in boxcar); Library of Congress (climbing into boxcar);
Library of Congress, photo by Russell Lee (hobo jungle); pp. 66-67—National Air and Space
Museum, Smithsonian Institution, 87-2489 (Roosevelt and Earhart); from the Collections of Henry
Ford Museum and Greenfield Village (B.98389-advertisement; B.112569-ballerinas);
© CORBIS, CB018346 (airplane); used with permission of Bettmann/CORBIS (miniature golf);
photo by John Gutmann (street baseball game); pp. 68-69—courtesy of the George Hoffman
family (CCC camp); Library of Congress (CCC ditch diggers; poster);
Franklin D. Roosevelt Library (Roosevelt at CCC camp).

Cover Background Illustration by Paul Bachem

**Library of Congress Cataloging-in-Publication Data**

Tripp, Valerie, 1951–
Kit saves the day : a summer story / by Valerie Tripp ;
illustrations, Walter Rane ; vignettes, Susan McAliley.

p.  cm.  —  (The American girls collection)

Summary: Tired of doing chores and longing for adventure during
the Great Depression, Kit meets a hobo and decides to hop a freight train.
ISBN 1-58485-025-6 — ISBN 1-58485-024-8 (pbk.)
1. Depressions—1929—Juvenile fiction.
[1. Depressions—1929—Fiction. 2. Tramps—Fiction.]
I. Rane, Walter, ill. II. McAliley, Susan, ill.
III. American girl (Middleton, Wis.) IV. Title. V. Series.
PZ7.T7363 Kh   2001   [Fic]—dc21   2001018511

FOR WALTER RANE, INGRID SLAMER, AND
CAITLIN WAITE, WHO BROUGHT KIT TO LIFE
SO ARTFULLY, WITH THANKS

# TABLE OF CONTENTS

**DAD**
*Kit's father, a
businessman facing
the problems of the
Great Depression.*

**MOTHER**
*Kit's mother, who takes
care of her family and
their home with strength
and determination.*

**KIT**
*A clever, resourceful
girl who helps her family
cope with the dark days
of the Depression.*

**CHARLIE**
*Kit's affectionate
and supportive
older brother.*

**AUNT
MILLIE**
*The lively and loving
woman who raised Dad.*

MRS. HOWARD
*Mother's garden club
friend, who is a guest in
the Kittredge home.*

STIRLING
HOWARD
*Mrs. Howard's son,
whose delicate health
hides surprising
strengths.*

WILL
SHEPHERD
*A young hobo from
Texas, who is befriended
by Kit and her family.*

# CHAPTER ONE

## STUCK

"Ya-hoo!"

Kit Kittredge whooped with joy. She flew into the kitchen waving an envelope over her head. "Look, everybody!" she shouted. "It's from Charlie!" Kit's mother, dad, and Aunt Millie gathered around her eagerly. A letter from Charlie was always a treat. "Here, Dad," Kit said. "You read it."

Mr. Kittredge dried his hands on the dish towel wrapped around his waist before he took the letter. It was a hot, sticky August afternoon, and the kitchen was steamy because the grownups were sterilizing glass jars in boiling water to prepare them for jams and preserves.

"'Dear Folks,'" Dad read aloud. "'I'm sitting on a patch of snow . . .'"

"Snow!" exclaimed Kit enviously.

"Shh!" shushed Mother and Aunt Millie.

Dad continued, "'. . . on a mountaintop here in Glacier National Park. There's nothing but blue sky and pine trees around me. This week, we're working on a stone wall next to a road called "Going-to-the-Sun Highway." It's hard, but all of us fellows are glad to have work to do. We have fun, too. I've told my baseball team that my kid sister Kit is the best catcher in Cincinnati! Well, break time's over. I'll write again soon. I miss you. I wish all of you could see how pretty Montana is. Love, Charlie.'"

For a moment after Dad finished reading, everyone just stood there grinning. It was as if Charlie had sent a brisk mountain breeze in his letter, a breeze that blew all the way from Glacier Park to stir the stifling air in the kitchen, refresh everyone, and lift their spirits. Then Kit saw Mother and Dad exchange a wistful look. *They miss Charlie,* she thought. Kit knew how they felt. She, too, missed Charlie and his jokes, his big, guffawing laugh, and the way he took the stairs two at a time. Charlie had been far away in Montana since June. He was working for the Civilian Conservation Corps, which was a program started by President Roosevelt to provide jobs for young men who were out of work because of the Depression.

"This is for you, Kit," said Dad. He handed Kit a photo of Charlie in a group of young men. They were in a forest, smiling broadly at the camera.

Kit saw a note on the back. "'Hey, Squirt!'" she read aloud. "'I thought you'd like this photo of me and my CCC buddies. Write and tell me what you're up to. XO, Charlie.'" Kit rose on her toes in delight. She loved writing! "I'll go make one of my newspapers for Charlie right now," she announced. She slipped the photo into her pocket and took off flying toward the hall.

"Kit!" said Mother. "Have you finished your chores?"

Kit crash-landed to a stop. "No," she admitted, "but—"

"Please do, dear," said Mother, "before you do anything else."

Aunt Millie added, "And please give the chickens fresh water. They'll be thirsty on a hot day like today."

Kit scowled, but none of the grown-ups noticed. They'd already turned back to their work. Clouds of steam rose from the pots on the stove, and the glass jars clinked and clanked in the boiling water.

"'Double, double toil and trouble; Fire burn and cauldron bubble,'" said Aunt Millie cheerfully, wiping her foggy eyeglasses on her apron.

Kit knew Aunt Millie was quoting the witches in a play by Shakespeare called *Macbeth*. Right now, Kit felt as low-down as a mean witch. She let the screen door slam shut behind her and stalked over to the chicken pen. The chickens usually greeted her with energetic squawking. But today they were under a listless spell because of the heat. They ignored Kit and didn't bother to cluck their thanks when she filled their water pan.

*I'm just a drudge,* Kit grumbled to herself, feeling cross that even the chickens seemed to take her for

granted. She picked up her broom and
went back to work beating the rug hung
over the clothesline. *Mop, sweep, scrub,
polish, do the laundry, wash the dishes, feed
the chickens, weed the garden—my chores never end!*

Dust and dirt billowed up off the rug and stuck
to Kit's sweaty face and arms so that she was soon
as spotty as an old brown toad. She kicked off her
sandals, which, like all of her clothes, were too
small. But freeing her feet did not cheer her up. The
more Kit thought about her situation, the crosser she
became. She'd *never* have time to write a newspaper
for Charlie. After beating the rug, she was supposed
to help Dad clean out the gutters. After that, it
would be time to help Mother cook and serve
dinner. And after dinner, there'd be the dishes to
wash, dry, and put away.

There would be *lots* of dishes, too. Eleven people
lived in Kit's house. A year ago, Mr. Kittredge had
lost his job because of the Depression, and Kit's
family had turned their home into a boarding house
to earn money. There were seven boarders now: two
nurses named Miss Hart and Miss Finney, a
musician named Mr. Peck, an elderly couple named

Mr. and Mrs. Bell, and a lady named Mrs. Howard and her son Stirling, who was exactly Kit's age. But even though the house was jam-packed with paying guests, and even though the Kittredges pinched every penny till it squealed, they still just eked out barely enough money to pay the bills month after month. It seemed to Kit that, just like chores, the Depression was never going to end.

Kit whacked the rug harder than was strictly necessary.

"Wow," said Stirling, crossing the yard toward Kit. "I wish your broom was a bat and the rug was a ball. That would have been a home run."

"And *that*," Kit said grimly as she walloped the rug again, "is as close as I'll get to swinging a baseball bat this summer."

Dust from the rug surrounded Stirling like a dirty cloud, but he didn't budge. He stood patiently, waiting for Kit to explain why she was so grumpy. Kit's dog Grace ambled over. Grace liked to be wherever a conversation was going on. She plunked herself down and drooled on Kit's kicked-off sandals.

"We had a letter from Charlie," Kit said. "He sent me this." Kit took Charlie's photo out of her pocket and gave it to Stirling. "Read the back."

Stirling did. Then he said, "Let's go make him a newspaper."

"I can't!" Kit exploded. "I have to do my dumb chores!"

Kit knew it was unfair to snap at Stirling. Chores weren't *his* fault. Besides, he worked hard, too. At the beginning of the summer, he'd surprised everyone by up and getting himself a job selling newspapers on a street corner. Stirling still looked like a pip-squeak, but he acted sturdier and more sure of himself. Kit thought it was because he had a real job out in the world and was earning money—just like Charlie, who sent home twenty-five of the thirty dollars he earned through the CCC every month.

"Sorry you can't write a newspaper for Charlie," said Stirling.

"Well, what would I write about anyway?" said Kit, putting the photo back in her pocket. "Dusting? The laundry? I'm not doing anything exciting. Charlie's the one who's having an adventure." Kit sighed and leaned on her broom. "The truth is," she admitted, "I'm jealous of Charlie." Lucky Charlie

was living in a place where there were mountain
peaks and hidden valleys, cool blue lakes and dark
green pines, rushing streams and thundering
waterfalls. By contrast, Kit's life was flat, colorless,
and humdrum. "I wish *I* could have an adventure,"
she said. "I'm tired of doing the same old chores. I
feel so bogged down, so *stuck*. I'd like to fly away
and escape."

"In that case," said Stirling, "I don't wish your
broom was a baseball bat. I wish it was a witch's
broom."

Kit laughed in spite of herself. She straddled the
broom and pretended to try to take off but remained,
of course, solidly planted on the ground. "I give up,"
she said. "Looks like my broom's stuck, too."

Kit slapped at a mosquito. Too late. Now there'd
be a bite on her neck, which was already sunburned
and itchy with sweat.

It was a few days later. Kit was in the
vegetable garden, moving slowly between
rows of tomato plants and picking the
ripest tomatoes off the vines. Aunt Millie

had declared today tomato harvest day. She'd decided that most of the tomatoes were ready to be preserved, and she did not want to waste one tomato—or one minute, either. She had rousted everyone out of bed at dawn and hurried them to work.

By now it was mid-morning. Kit and Stirling were outside picking. Mother was in the kitchen stewing and preserving. Dad was carrying jars of preserved tomatoes to the basement. Aunt Millie buzzed back and forth, inside and outside, bossing both pickers and preservers. "We'll be glad for all this work come winter," she said happily. "Think of the money we'll save by eating food we've grown ourselves. And it'll remind us of summer. When we eat these tomatoes, we'll remember what Shakespeare calls 'summer's honey breath'!"

Kit and Stirling smiled at each other through the tomato plants. They were used to the way Aunt Millie quoted Shakespeare. She'd been a teacher for many years, and she couldn't help teaching wherever she was.

As usual, Aunt Millie and Shakespeare were quite right. The air *did* feel like honey—liquid, heavy, and sticky. Even so, Kit was grateful to be outdoors. The day before she'd practically melted in the suffocating kitchen helping Aunt Millie make peach jam. Kit had stirred the pot of thick goo on the stove until her hand was glued to the spoon with peach juice and her feet were pasted to the floor with jam. Today, in the garden, there was at least a sluggish breeze rustling the limp leaves every so often. The tomatoes glowed red and were so plump they seemed about to burst their smooth skins. Each one had a satisfying heft when Kit held it in her hand. Her basket was heavy when she stood up and carried it to Aunt Millie, who took it inside.

Kit had knelt down and gone back to picking when Grace barked a friendly bark. Grace was supposed to be a guard dog, but she seemed to think that anyone who came to the house had come only to admire *her* and therefore should be welcomed politely. Kit poked her head up above the tomatoes.

"Hey," said someone.

Kit turned and saw a stranger standing at the edge of the garden. It was a teenage boy in a dusty cap and stained, baggy, roughly patched trousers.

"Hey, yourself," Kit said.

*"Hey, yourself," Kit said.*

Now Stirling raised his head, too. The teenage boy grinned such a big, wide grin that Kit and Stirling had to smile back. Kit knew he was a hobo. He had the same scruffy, scrawny look as all the hoboes and tramps who came to the house looking for a handout or a job to do in return for food.

The boy bent down to scratch Grace's back. He nodded toward the garden. "The tomatoes look good," he said. Just then the screen door opened and Aunt Millie came out. The boy's grin disappeared. He shot up straight, pulled his cap off, and pushed his shaggy, dark hair out of his eyes. "How do, ma'am," he said. His voice was respectful and a little wary. He sounded as if he half expected Aunt Millie to shoo him away.

But Kit knew Aunt Millie would never shoo away a stray *dog*, much less a stray boy. "What can I do for you, son?" Aunt Millie asked.

"Well, ma'am," said the boy. "I was just saying to the young lady yonder what a good crop of tomatoes you've got. Your string beans are ready to be picked, too. I'd be glad to help. Looks like maybe you could use a hand."

"Looks like maybe *you* could use a bite to eat," said Aunt Millie. "You're as skinny as a string bean yourself!"

The boy grinned his wide, wonderful grin again. "I'd be obliged," he said. "But not until after I work."

Aunt Millie smiled. "What's your name, son?" she asked.

"William Shepherd," answered the boy. "But nowadays, most folks call me Texas Will, or just plain Will."

"All right, just plain Will," said Aunt Millie. She handed him an empty basket. "You can help Kit and Stirling with the picking. Mind, there won't be any pay in it for you. None but lunch, anyway."

"That'll do fine, ma'am," said Will. He bent over a tomato plant and went straight to work.

"I'll tell the folks inside there'll be one more for lunch," said Aunt Millie. She went back into the kitchen.

Kit was burning with curiosity about Will. She had hundreds of questions to ask him. Also, she wanted to hear Will talk more. She liked the way he pronounced his name "wheel" and called Aunt Millie "may-um."

"Are you from Texas?" Kit asked.

"Yep," Will answered without stopping his work.

"How'd you get as far as Cincinnati?" Stirling asked.

"Riding the rails, mostly," said Will. "Hopping freights. I ride freight trains for free by jumping into empty boxcars."

"Aren't you kind of young?" Kit asked. "To be a hobo, I mean."

"I'm fifteen," said Will. "There are lots of hoboes my age, some even younger." He glanced at Kit. "Girls not much older than you ride the rails."

"They do?" Kit asked, fascinated.

"Yep," said Will.

*Gosh!* thought Kit. *What a life that must be. Very exciting—and very **unstuck**!*

# JUST PLAIN WILL

Will was a quick, quiet worker. With his help, all the ripest tomatoes were picked by lunchtime. Mother brought a tray of sandwiches outside, and Dad brought a pitcher of milk so that they could have lunch on the shady back porch. Will looked at the sandwiches as if he could devour them all. Kit knew how he felt. She was always hungry herself. Mother often teased that Kit was eating them out of house and home! But before they could eat, Aunt Millie brought out a basin of hot water, a bar of soap, and a hand towel.

"Wash up, children," she ordered Kit, Stirling, and Will.

Kit and Stirling washed quickly. But Will pushed up his sleeves, plunged his hands into the hot water, and sighed with pleasure. He lathered up his hands, cupped them, and scooped up handful after handful of water to wash his face, letting the warm, soapy water run down his neck. Then he scrubbed his arms up to his elbows and dried off with the towel. Water drops glistened on his hair. Kit realized soap and hot water were luxuries hoboes like Will probably didn't often see.

"You're a good worker, Will," said Aunt Millie as she filled his milk glass. "You know what you're doing in a garden."

"I ought to," said Will, with his winning grin. "My family had a farm back in Texas."

"Don't you miss your family?" asked Mother.

"I do, ma'am," answered Will. "And I miss the farm. It used to be beautiful. My father grew wheat. In the spring, the fields looked like a green ocean. Then hard times came. My father couldn't make any money selling his wheat. After that, it seemed like nature turned against us, because it never rained. The wheat dried up, dead and brown. It cracked under your feet when you walked through the fields, and the soil was nothing but dust." Will sighed. "A couple of big wind storms came and just blew the farm away. Scattered it. My family's gone, too. They packed up everything and left."

"How come you didn't go with them?" Kit asked Will.

"Kit," Mother scolded gently. "That's a personal question."

"It's all right, ma'am," said Will. He looked at Kit. "See, my father is a proud man. It about killed him when he lost the farm and couldn't feed us anymore. I knew he hated having me see him brought so low. And I knew I was one more mouth he couldn't feed, one more pair of feet he couldn't buy shoes for. So when my family packed up to leave Texas, I made up my mind to go off on my own. I figured it was time for me to take care of myself."

Kit understood. She felt guilty about her appetite and about growing so much and so fast that she was always needing bigger clothes and shoes, too. She felt like Alice in Wonderland, who suddenly grew so big she filled the house! Except that Alice's clothes grew, too, which was very convenient. Kit's arms and legs dangled out of most of her clothes as if she were a gangly daddy longlegs. Kit thought Will was brave and noble to have left his family so that he wasn't an expense to them anymore.

"Did you run away?" Stirling asked.

"Yep," said Will. "I've been most everywhere since then. I follow the crops. I went north to harvest potatoes in the fall, south to pick walnuts in the winter, and east to pick strawberries in the spring. Now I'm on my way west to Oregon for the apple harvest."

Dad spoke, and Kit heard something that sounded like envy in his voice. "You've seen a lot of country for someone your age," he said to Will.

"Yes, sir, and met a lot of people, too," said Will. "But none kinder than you folks." He stood up and put his cap back on his head. "Thank you for the fine lunch. I'll be on my way now."

Dad glanced at Mother and Aunt Millie. All three seemed to come to an agreement without saying a word.

Kit was happy when she heard Dad say, "Just a minute, Will. We'll be up to our elbows picking and preserving tomorrow, too. We'd be glad to have your help, if you'd like to stay. We can't pay you, but we can feed you and give you a place to sleep."

"I'll give you a haircut, too," said Aunt Millie. "You look like you haven't had one since you left home."

Will's grin lit his whole face. "Thanks," he said. "I'd like that. I'll stay."

"Good!" said Kit. "You can tell us about all the places you've been!"

At first, Will was shy at dinner. But he soon grew comfortable and talkative. All the boarders liked him. Mother beamed at him, and Aunt Millie gave him extra-large portions of food. Dad, who was always interested in places he had never been, asked Kit to bring the atlas to the table. He opened the atlas to a map of the United States so that Will could show them where he was from in Texas and point out all the places he'd been before he came to Ohio. Kit found Glacier Park, Montana, on the map and told Will about Charlie and the

19

work he was doing there with the CCC.

After dinner, Mr. Peck played his bass fiddle while Mrs. Bell played the piano, and Will taught them all to dance the Texas two-step.

"We haven't had that much fun since Charlie left," Kit said as she led Will outside, carrying a lantern, blankets, and a pillow. Will had chosen not to sleep in the house. "Where do you want these?" she asked. "In the garage? Or on the porch?"

"I'll sleep on the ground," said Will. "I'm not used to a roof anymore. Makes me feel too closed in."

"All right," said Kit. "Good night."

"Good night," said Will.

As Kit climbed up to her attic room, she thought that Will was wise to be outdoors. "It's so stuffy in here!" she sighed, flopping onto her bed.

Aunt Millie, who shared Kit's room, looked up from her book of Shakespeare's sonnets. "What can't be cured must be endured," she said.

Kit fanned herself with her hand. "The house feels hot and crowded to me tonight," she complained. "It's getting on my nerves."

"Anyone can get along in a palace, dear child,"

said Aunt Millie. "Living squashed together is a true test of character."

Kit loved Aunt Millie, but sometimes she thought it would be nice to be *alone*. She clicked on her gooseneck lamp and opened her favorite book, *Robin Hood and His Adventures*, hoping that reading would soothe and absorb her as it usually did. But the  imaginary adventures of Robin Hood and his merry men didn't interest her tonight. Instead, Kit found herself staring at the photo of Charlie and his CCC buddies, which she'd propped up in front of her lamp. Kit's thoughts flew far and wide, out into the velvety black night, to Montana where Charlie was, and to the faraway places Will had been. What she longed for was a *real* adventure of her own.

The next day, Kit was hanging sheets on the clothesline. A hot, sultry wind lifted the sheets so that they fluttered like moist white wings around her. Aunt Millie had set up an open-air barbershop next to the clothesline. She'd cut Stirling's hair and now she was at work on Will.

"I appreciate this, ma'am," he said. "I don't meet
barbers in the jungle."

"What's the jungle?" asked Stirling.

"That's what we hoboes call our camps,"
explained Will. "A jungle is usually close to the
railroad tracks. There's one here in Cincinnati near
Union Station, right next to the river."

"Do you cook over a campfire?" asked Kit
dreamily. "And tell stories about the places you've
been? And sing songs, and sleep out under the
stars?"

"Well . . ." Will began as if he were starting a

long explanation. Then he seemed to change his mind. He answered simply, "Yep."

"I've seen some of those camps," Aunt Millie said, snipping through Will's thick hair with her sharp scissors. "They look mighty uncomfortable! Hot in summer, cold in winter, wet in the rain, and buggy to boot."

"Maybe," said Kit. "But there'd be no rugs to beat or gutters to clean. And you could just come and go as you pleased. It sounds fine to me."

Aunt Millie shook her head. "A wanderer's life is lonely and hard," she said. "I believe most people are good-hearted, but not everyone's kind to hoboes." She untied the cloth she'd put around Will's shoulders and shook the hair off it. "You're done, just plain Will," she said. "And much improved, if I do say so myself."

"Thank you, ma'am," said Will as Aunt Millie went inside. Will stood and brushed off his pants. "I sure am glad I stopped here," he said to Kit and Stirling.

"Why *did* you stop at our house?" asked Kit. "How'd you know we'd be nice?"

"I saw the sign," said Will.

"What sign?" asked Kit and Stirling together.

"Come on," Will said, tilting his head toward the fence. "I'll show you."

Kit and Stirling followed Will to the corner of the yard where the fence met the street.

"Look," said Will. On the fencepost, someone had drawn a sketch of a cat.

"That sign means a kind-hearted woman lives here."

"Oh!" exclaimed Kit, enchanted. "Are there other signs, too?"

"Yep," said Will. "Lots of 'em. They're a secret code that we hoboes use to tell each other what to expect in the places we go. Usually, the sign is scratched on a fence or drawn on a building or a sidewalk with chalk or coal."

"Can you show us more?" asked Kit.

"Sure," said Will. Stirling, who liked to draw, always had a pencil stub and a piece of scrap paper in his pocket. He gave the pencil and paper to Will now.

Will drew one horizontal line. "One line means it's a doubtful place, better not stop there," he said. He added three more lines and explained, "But four

24

lines means that the lady of the house will give you food if you do chores." Will drew a circle with two arrows pointing out of it. "This means 'get out fast,' and this . . ." he drew a big V, "means 'pretend to be sick.'"

"Why would you do that?" asked Stirling.

"If you pretend to be sick, folks will help you and feed you," said Will.

"But isn't it lying to fake an illness?" asked Kit.

"I suppose it is," said Will. "But on the road . . . well, sometimes you have to do whatever it takes to survive."

"Do you ever . . . steal?" asked Kit.

Will took a deep breath. "Let me ask you this," he said. "Say you work hard all morning helping a farmer harvest potatoes, and at the end, he gives you two wormy ones for your labor. If you slip two more potatoes in your pockets without telling him, is it stealing?"

Kit and Stirling didn't answer.

"Hunger changes the rules somewhat," said Will. He drew a circle and a square and put a dot in the middle of each. "This is the sign you'd leave on the stingy farmer's fencepost. It means a bad-tempered man lives there."

Kit nudged Stirling. "I bet *that* sign is outside Uncle Hendrick's house," she said. Kit's uncle lived downtown. He was well-to-do, very stingy, and often mean.

"Signs aren't the only way hoboes help each other," said Will. "When hoboes ride into town on the train, we go to the jungle. Then we spread out and look for chores to do for food. Maybe I sweep out a store and the storekeeper gives me a couple of onions. I bring them back to the jungle and put them together with everyone else's food to make a hobo stew. See, onions alone aren't so great. But add 'em to a pot of stew and there's more food for all, and it tastes better, too."

"Hobo stew," said Kit, savoring the words. "I wish I could try some."

Will said his thank-yous and good-byes early that afternoon, explaining that he planned to spend the night in the jungle near Union Station and then hop a freight headed west the next day. Kit was very sorry to see him go.

"It's duller than ever around here," she griped to Stirling later as they took the dry sheets off the clothesline and put them in the laundry basket. "Will's the only interesting thing that's happened to us all summer."

Stirling agreed. "I liked hearing about the jungle and the hoboes," he said. He patted his pocket where he kept his pencil stub and scrap paper. "I liked the secret signs Will taught us, too."

"Didn't that hobo stew sound good?" asked Kit. All at once, she gasped. "Oh, no!" she exclaimed. "We didn't give Will anything for the stew!"

Kit and Stirling looked at each other in dismay. Then Kit had an idea. "You know what?" she said eagerly. "I bet if we asked, Mother and Aunt Millie would give us some food. We could bring it down to the jungle near Union Station and give it to Will to put in the hobo stew."

"I don't—" Stirling began doubtfully.

"Listen, Stirling," Kit interrupted. "Remember that stingy farmer with the wormy potatoes Will told us about?"

Stirling nodded.

"Well, we're worse than that farmer if we don't give Will some of the tomatoes and beans he picked," said Kit. "We owe Will some food for the stew. He worked hard helping us, didn't he?"

Stirling nodded again.

"Besides, aren't you dying to see the jungle?" said Kit. "I am!" She hoisted the laundry basket onto her hip and spoke with a mixture of determination and excitement. "As soon as I finish my chores, I'll talk to the grownups. And then we'll go find Will."

# THE HOBO JUNGLE

"No, Grace," Kit said. "You can't come with us to the jungle. Stay."

Grace sighed. She sank down, her ears puddling around her head and her droopy eyes looking sad. Kit was sorry, but Grace didn't move very fast on her short legs and her splayed feet that pointed out like a duck's. And Kit was in a hurry. She and Stirling were just setting forth and it was already late afternoon. Finishing her chores had taken longer than Kit had expected.

Talking to the grownups had, too. Mrs. Howard had said that the jungle was dangerous, probably full of thugs and murderers! But luckily, Aunt Millie had persuaded her that most hoboes were just folks

who were down on their luck, and that going to the
jungle would be a generous, educational thing for
Kit and Stirling to do. Mrs. Howard fussed, but she
gave in after Stirling promised not to eat any of the
hobo stew. Otherwise, she was sure he'd come down
with some dreadful disease.

Now, finally, Kit and Stirling were
on their way with a flour-sack bag full
of food that Aunt Millie had packed.
There were fresh tomatoes and beans
from the garden, a can of stewed tomatoes, and a
can of milk. Kit's stomach was fluttery. She was an
honest girl, and she admitted to herself that she
wanted to bring food to the hoboes not just out of
kindness, but also out of curiosity. The part of her
that was a writer was always intrigued by new ex-
periences. At last, she'd have something interesting
to write about in her newspaper for Charlie. She'd
notice everything about the jungle. And no matter
what Mrs. Howard said, *she'd* taste the hobo stew!

It was not a long walk to Union Station from
the Kittredges' house. Very shortly, Kit and Stirling
passed the huge front of the train station. They
continued past the rail yards to the riverbank

underneath the trestle bridge. There, almost hidden
in a little grove of trees and low bushes, was a
cleared-out space of bare ground with a smoky fire
in the middle of it.

"We're here," breathed Kit to Stirling. "This is
the jungle."

Kit and Stirling looked around with wide eyes.
Somehow, the jungle was not as comfortable-looking
as Kit had imagined. There were a few tumbledown
shelters made of old boards leaning against trees
and a few dirty tents that sagged tiredly. The people
looked tired, too. Some were washing their clothes

in the river and then spreading them on bushes to dry. One man was shaving, standing at a cracked mirror hung from a tree branch. But most of the hoboes were stretched out on the ground, hard asleep, their hats covering their faces. Someone was playing a soft, haunting tune on a harmonica. The air smelled of wood smoke, coffee, and stew.

Kit was glad to see Will coming toward her.

"Hey," said Will. "Kit and Stirling, what are you doing here?"

Kit took the food out of the sack. "We came to give you this food for the hobo stew," she said. "Sorry we forgot before."

Will grinned. "Well, thanks," he said.

Will used a sharp rock to open the cans. He lifted the lid from the pot, added the canned tomatoes and the fresh tomatoes and beans from the garden, stirred the stew, and gave Kit a taste. It was very spicy. In a moment, a woman came to the fire and filled three bowls from the pot. Kit was sadly surprised when she saw that the woman was bringing the stew to three very small, very hungry-looking children. One of the children was practically a baby. Will gave the young mother the can of milk.

Then he looked at Kit's face. "What's the matter?" he asked.

Kit said slowly, "I didn't expect to see little kids here." Kit had assumed that hoboes were people like Will who'd *chosen* to live an adventurous life on the road. Now she understood that most of them were poor, lost people—families with tiny babies, even— who had once been settled and respectable but now, because of the Depression, had no place to call home.

Kit saw that the young mother's husband was asleep. He'd tied his shoes to his wrist. "Why'd he do that?" Kit asked Will quietly.

"He's afraid someone will steal his shoes while he's asleep," explained Will. "A hobo's shoes are his most valuable possession. Can't get anywhere without 'em. Men gamble for shoes, and fight for 'em, too."

Kit looked around at the other hoboes. They were wearing street shoes, tennis shoes, old rubber boots, shoes with pieces of tire nailed to the bottom, mismatched hiking boots, even rags wrapped around their feet and legs and tied on with rope. One boy had taken off a huge old pair of four-buckle

galoshes. He wore two pairs of socks, and he was
stuffing crumpled newspaper into the toes of the
galoshes to make them fit. Another man was
repairing his boots, which were clearly too small for
him. When Kit saw his feet, she was heartsick and a
little ashamed of herself. The way her sandals
pinched her toes was nothing compared to the way
this man's poor feet were rubbed raw and bleeding.

Kit's attention was suddenly distracted by a
noisy group of men arriving in the jungle. They
greeted the others and squatted down by the fire.

"A freight train must've pulled in," Will
explained to Kit and Stirling.

One of the younger men looked up."Well, if it
isn't Texas Will," he said, smirking. He pronounced
Will "whee-yull," making fun of Will's accent.

"Hello, Lex," said Will. Kit could tell that Will
did not like Lex.

"Who's this?" Lex asked, pointing at Kit and
Stirling.

"They're friends of mine," said Will. "They live
just north of here."

"So, kids," Lex drawled, "I bet Will has told you
all about me, his old friend Lex, and how I'm the

world's best at hopping freights."

Kit and Stirling shook their heads no.

"He didn't?" said Lex, pretending to be surprised. "Well, come on then. I'll show you how good I am." Lex stood up. "Better yet, I'll teach you how to hop a freight. What do you say?"

"Leave 'em alone, Lex," said Will.

But Lex ignored Will and spoke straight to Kit. "There's nothing to it," he said. "The train I just got off is heading north. We'll hop it and get off at the first stop, still within the city limits. It'll be a ride toward home for you and your little buddy there." He tilted his head toward Stirling.

Everyone was quiet, waiting to see what Kit would do. She knew Lex was a braggart and not to be trusted. But a chance to hop a freight was a chance for a *real* adventure.

"Lex is all talk, Kit," said Will. "Don't let him bamboozle you."

Lex still spoke to Kit. "I'm not talking you into anything, am I, missie?" he said in a wheedling voice. "You'd like to try it. I can tell by the look in your eyes that you're curious. Oh, but maybe you're afraid. Is that it? You scared?"

"I am not!" said Kit hotly. "I want to do it."

"No, Kit," said Will. "Hopping freights is dangerous. It's against the—"

But Kit was not listening. "*You* hop freights all the time," she cut in. "And you told me that lots of girls my age do it, too. How dangerous can it be?" Kit lowered her voice and spoke earnestly. "Don't you see, Will?" she asked. "This is my one chance to do something exciting. I *can't* let it go by." She turned to Stirling. "Listen," she said, "you don't have to come."

Stirling looked at Kit with his huge, pure gray eyes. "Yes, I do," he said.

"Let's go, then," said Lex impatiently. "The train will be leaving soon."

"This is a bad idea, Kit," said Will, frowning. "But if you're so set on it, I'm coming, too. I've got to be sure you get home safely."

Kit, Stirling, and a reluctant Will followed Lex along the riverbank, under the trestle bridge, and up a hill. They skirted the edge of the rail yard, making their way between huge freight cars and over a tangle of rails. Kit was soon so twisted around that she had no idea what direction she was headed in.

At last, Lex stopped. He pointed to a red boxcar whose door was open. It was part of a train that was so long that Kit couldn't see the engine or the caboose.

"We'll jump into that boxcar," Lex said. "But we have to wait until the train moves out of the rail yard before we do."

Kit's heart beat fast with excitement while they waited for the train to move. Finally, with a slow hiss of steam, the train's wheels began to turn and the train chugged toward them, gathering speed. Lex ran along next to it with Kit, Stirling, and Will following him. Then Lex grabbed onto a metal ladder attached to the boxcar and, in a move as smooth as a cat's, swung himself up and into the open door. He made it look easy.

Kit and Stirling ran next to each other, staying even with the train. Then Stirling tripped. He started to fall forward, and for one sickening second Kit was afraid he'd be crushed under the wheels of the train. But Will caught him from behind, grabbed him by the scruff of the neck and the seat of his pants, and tossed him headfirst onto the train as if he were a sack of potatoes. Then Will swung himself up into the car, too.

The train was moving faster and faster. Kit was a good runner, but she had to run with all her might to keep up with the red boxcar. Will knelt down in the open door of the boxcar and reached out his hand to Kit.

"Grab my hand," he shouted over the noise of the train.

Kit put on a burst of speed. She stretched her arm out, reaching, reaching, *reaching* for Will's hand. At last, she caught it. Will lifted her up so that she dangled, then swung her so she flew through the air into the boxcar. Kit thudded against the hard wooden floor as she landed.

"Are you okay?" Will asked her.

Kit was too out of breath to talk, so she just nodded. Eagerly, she scrambled to her feet and stood by the open door. The wind blew her hair every which way, smoke stung her eyes, and cinders smudged her face, but she didn't care. Faster and faster the train rushed along the track, until the world outside was just a blur. Kit was exhilarated. She'd never moved so fast! She'd never felt so free! For a second, for a heartbeat,

Kit wished the train would never stop.

Then Stirling tugged on her arm. "Kit!" he said urgently. "Lex led us to the wrong train. We're not going north, toward home. We're going south, across the river. Look!"

Kit stuck her head out. Sure enough, the train was barreling across the trestle bridge, the tracks spooling out behind it, the river flowing below. With every click of the wheels, Cincinnati grew smaller and home was farther away.

Kit whirled around. "Lex!" she shouted, searching for his face in the dimness of the boxcar. "Did you trick us on purpose?"

Lex didn't answer. Because just then, the brakes slammed on and the train *screeched* to a stop. Kit held on tight to the door to keep from falling. She looked out to see where they were. The train had crossed the bridge. It was stopped in a wooded area where a dirt road crossed the railroad tracks. Kit saw lots of men coming toward the train.

"This is trouble!" muttered Lex. He knocked Kit out of his way, leaped out of the boxcar, and disappeared into the trees.

Will held a finger to his lips and gestured for Kit and Stirling to stand up and press themselves against the wall behind him. Outside, Kit heard angry voices and the sound of fists and sticks pounding on the boxcars.

"Will!" Kit whispered. "What's happening?"

"The train's been stopped by railroad bulls," answered Will. "Bulls are men the railroad hires to throw hoboes off the trains." He pulled off his cap. "Put this on," he said to Kit. "I don't want them to know you're a girl."

"Why?" Kit started to ask. But suddenly, she was blinded by a flashlight aimed straight into her eyes. Will and Stirling froze in the light, too.

"All right!" growled a harsh voice. "Are you bums going to come out by yourselves, or do I have to come in there and toss you out like trash?"

"Come on!" ordered another voice. "Out!"

Will jumped out of the boxcar. He turned to help Kit and Stirling, but one of the railroad bulls shoved him aside, grasped the two smaller children each by an arm, and jerked them out so roughly that they fell onto the dusty, rocky ground. Kit stood. She tried to brush the dirt off her overalls, but it just smeared.

*Suddenly, Kit was blinded by a flashlight aimed straight into her eyes.*

She wiped her hands on the seat of her pants.

Outside the boxcar was a scene of scary confusion. Railroad bulls swarmed over the train, hauling hoboes out of the boxcars, shouting, and pushing the hoboes into a double line. The railroad bulls carried stout sticks and bats. Some even had guns. Stirling stood right next to Kit, and Will stood in front of them, trying to shield them as best he could from the bulls.

But it was no use. One of the bulls rapped Kit sharply on the back of her legs with his club. "Line up, you bum!" the bull ordered.

Kit spoke fiercely. "I'm not a bum," she said.

"Hah!" scoffed the man. He eyed Kit's filthy overalls, dirty hands, and sooty face. "You look like a bum to me. Get in line. Be quick about it." He pushed Kit into line between Stirling and Will.

"Where are they taking us?" Kit asked Will as they walked forward.

"To town," said Will. "Keep my cap on your head. Hide your hair. If they see that you're a girl, they'll separate us at the jail."

"*Jail?*" gasped Kit. "Why are we going to jail? We didn't do anything wrong. We're not criminals!"

"Hopping a freight is against the law," said Will. "I tried to tell you, but you wouldn't listen. And they put us in jail so that we won't beg or panhandle in their town. We'll spend the night in a cell. In the morning, they'll put us in a truck and drive us out of town."

*Spend the night in jail?* thought Kit miserably. She looked behind her to see if there was any way to escape. But the double line of hoboes, about twenty in all, was closely guarded by bulls on all sides. The pitiful parade left the woods and entered a town called Spencerville. As the hoboes passed, the townspeople stared and frowned at them with dislike and distrust.

The jail was a squat brick building that faced the town square. Its walls were thick, and its front windows had bars. Kit and the others were herded inside. "Turn your pockets inside out," the sheriff ordered them.

Kit and Will had empty pockets, the sheriff let Stirling keep his scrap of paper and pencil stub. Then all the hoboes were crowded into a small, square room. It had a concrete floor and one tiny window, but no furniture. The hoboes filed in silently and sat on the hard floor or slouched tiredly against the walls. Kit stood close to Will and Stirling. The wall was cold against her back. Tears pricked her eyes as she watched the door swing shut and heard it lock with a hollow, horrifying *clang*.

# DO SOMETHING

Kit shivered.

"Don't be afraid," said Will softly.

"I'm not," said Kit, though she was. "I'm mad. We've got to get out of here. We've got to *do* something."

Stirling gave her an earnest look, but he said nothing.

Soon, there was a loud rattle and clatter in the hall. The door opened and the sheriff announced, "Dinner." All the hoboes stood and formed a line.

They were each given a mug of water and a tin plate with a cold boiled potato, a spoonful of beans, and a slice of soggy, moldy bread on it. Though Kit was hungry, she had to force herself to eat. The food smelled sour. It stuck in her throat so that she had to wash it down with the rusty-tasting water.

After dinner, the sheriff brought wash basins of cold water, bars of hard soap, and newspapers for towels for the hoboes to use to wash up. Kit gathered her courage and went to the sheriff.

"Please, sir," she said. "There's been a mistake. My friends and I aren't hoboes. My parents don't have a phone, but please let me call my Uncle Hendrick back in Cincinnati. He'll tell my parents and they'll come get us."

The sheriff crossed his arms over his chest. "If you have relatives in Cincinnati," he said, "what were you doing on the train? You bums! Always making up stories, like you've got an uncle who'll help you." He shook his head. "You think I believe that lie?"

"Please let me phone," said Kit. "You'll see I'm telling the truth."

"Hmph!" the sheriff snorted. "Where's your money for the call?"

"Well," said Kit. "I don't have any money. But—"

"Of course you don't," interrupted the sheriff. He laughed a mean laugh. "Nice try, boy. You're a good panhandler. But I've seen too many of you beggars to fall for your tricks. Where would I be if I let every tramp who asked me make a free phone call? In the poorhouse, that's where."

Kit stamped her foot. "I'm not a beggar!" she said.

"That's enough, boy!" said the sheriff. "Don't you get sassy! And take your hat off when you're speaking to me." Before Kit could stop him, he snatched Will's cap off her head. "Look at you," he snarled as he tossed the cap at her. "A girl! I *knew* you were a liar. Come with me. I'm going to put you in a separate cell."

"No!" said Kit furiously. She did not want to be separated from Will and Stirling. She struggled against the sheriff, but he was too strong for her. He held her tightly by the arm and pulled her along behind him.

Just before she passed through the door, Stirling yanked hard on her sleeve. Kit looked at him. He held up his scrap of paper, and on it, Kit saw:

*Kit knew it was one of the hobo signs. **But which one?**
she thought frantically. **What does it mean?***

Kit knew it was one of the hobo signs. *But which one?* she thought frantically. *What does it mean?* Suddenly, she remembered.

Kit bent forward and grabbed her stomach with her free hand. "Ohhh," she groaned. She tugged on the sheriff's arm and slumped against the wall. "Ohhh, my stomach. Please, sir, I feel sick." It wasn't a lie. The dinner *was* churning in her queasy stomach. Kit groaned again and held her hand over her mouth. "Please, let me go to the bathroom!"

"Oh, all right!" barked the sheriff, exasperated. He pointed. "In there."

Kit skittered into the bathroom. The second the door closed behind her, she looked around wildly, thinking, *Is there a way out? Oh, there has to be!* Then, high up the wall, she saw a little window. It was much too small for a grown person to fit through, but—

*Bang, bang!* The sheriff hammered on the door, growling, "Hurry up!"

"Yes, sir," Kit answered. Silently, carefully, she climbed up on the sink and opened the window. She poked her head and shoulders out, hoisted herself up, and slithered through, landing hard on the ground below. Kit scrambled to her feet. She leaned against the wall of the jail and allowed herself one shaky breath. Then she took off running. There was not a moment to lose. The sheriff would soon realize that she was gone.

*Oh, please don't let anyone see me,* she prayed as she ran.

But Kit had gone only a few yards when she heard, "Hey, you! Stop!" She looked over her shoulder. Men outside the jail had spotted her and were chasing after her, shouting, "Come back, you!" Kit ran as fast as she could, trying desperately to get away from the footsteps she could hear close behind her. A rough hand grabbed her shoulder. "Gotcha!" a man panted.

"No!" shrieked Kit. She wrenched her shoulder out of his grasp. The man lost his balance and fell behind her with a heavy thud. This time Kit didn't look back. She ran for all she was worth, pelting down the dirt road out of Spencerville, toward the railroad tracks. *Home,* she thought. *I've got to get home and get help for Stirling and Will!*

On and on Kit ran. Finally, up ahead, she saw the railroad tracks, shining silver, sharp as lightning in the darkness. She trotted next to them a short distance. Then she stopped dead. *Oh, no,* she thought. Below her was the river and looming above her was the railroad trestle bridge. It wasn't a solid bridge with a road on it. Instead, it was made of crisscrossed metal girders that looked like the strands of a gigantic spiderweb spun across the river. The train tracks that crossed the bridge were supported by wooden railroad ties with big gaps between them. *How will I ever cross this bridge?* Kit worried. *Jump from tie to tie? Balance on a rail as if it were a tightrope? If only there were another way to cross the river! If only there were another way home!*

But Kit had no choice. Slowly, she walked toward the bridge. She saw that there was a narrow catwalk, two boards wide, that ran alongside the train tracks. Kit took a deep breath. Gingerly, she put one foot on the catwalk to see if it would hold her weight. It did, so she eased her other foot onto it, too. The catwalk boards were spattered with oil, which made them slippery. Kit stood up straight, holding her arms out for balance. She tried not to look down. She tried not to hear the rushing river below. She knew that if she slipped, she might fall between the girders, and the river would sweep her away. Very cautiously, she slid one foot forward, then the other. *I can do it,* she said to herself. *I can cross this bridge. I **have** to.*

Clouds covered the moon, making it so Kit couldn't see far ahead. The bridge seemed to disappear into nothingness. All Kit could do was put one foot slowly, carefully, fearfully in front of the other and walk forward. The boards of the catwalk were uneven, and Kit stubbed her toe and stumbled, almost falling. *Just walk,* she urged herself. *Keep going.* Step by scary step, Kit inched her way along the catwalk until she was in the middle of the bridge. *I'm halfway across now,* she realized. *There's no turning back.*

Suddenly, the boards began to tremble under her feet. An eerie, mournful whistle pierced the air. It seemed to cut right through Kit.

"Oh, no!" she shrieked. A train was coming straight toward her and there was nowhere to go.

*I'm trapped!* thought Kit. Desperately, Kit did the only thing she could. She flung herself down on her stomach and stretched herself flat against the catwalk. She held onto the boards with both hands,

*Beneath her, the boards rattled and bounced, as if trying to toss her off into the water below. Kit held on for dear life.*

53

pressed her face into the splintery, oily wood, and closed her eyes. With a howling *whoosh!* the train pushed the air in front of it. With a monstrous force, it shook the bridge violently. With a deafening roar, it thundered past, just a few feet from Kit. She could feel its hot, fiery breath on her back. Beneath her, the boards rattled and bounced, as if trying to toss her off into the water below. Kit held on for dear life.

Then, as suddenly as it had appeared, the train was gone, screaming off into the dark. For a moment, Kit couldn't move. Then she spoke to herself sternly. *Get up. Get up and go.* Slowly, she lifted her face. Her fingers had gripped the boards so tightly that they ached when she let go. She pushed herself to her knees and, shakily, she stood. On wobbly legs, she made herself take one step forward, then another, and another. *I've got to get home,* she told herself over and over again. *I've got to get help for Stirling and Will.*

The bridge and the darkness seemed endless. But after a long, weary time, Kit blinked. *Are those lights?* she wondered, squinting at pinpoints that danced ahead of her. *It's the city!* she realized. Kit longed to quicken her steps, but she knew that would be dangerous. She had to hold herself back, force herself to walk slowly and carefully, until at last her feet were on solid ground and the bridge was behind her. Kit was so relieved that she wanted to collapse, but she couldn't allow herself to stop. She pushed on, past the rail yards, past Union Station, and through the city streets. The short, easy route she and Stirling had traveled on their way to the hoboes' jungle earlier that day felt long and difficult going the other way now. Kit was so footsore and tired that it took all of her strength to put one foot in front of the other.

As she trudged up the last hill to home, Kit's heart dragged as much as her feet. *Why did I hop that freight?* she thought. *How could I have been so stupid?* Desperate as she was to get home, Kit dreaded facing Mother, Dad, Aunt Millie, and Stirling's mother. *They'll be so angry!* she thought.

When at last Kit saw her house ahead of her, she broke into a run, and hot tears spilled out of her eyes. "Dad! Mother!" she called out, wiping the tears from her cheeks.

The front door opened and yellow light poured out across the lawn. Dad, Mother,

Aunt Millie, and Mrs. Howard rushed outside together, and Dad ran forward to catch Kit in his arms.

"Where have you been?" he asked. "Are you all right? Mr. Peck went down to the jungle to find you. We've been frantic! What's happened?"

"Where's Stirling?" asked Mrs. Howard.

For a moment, Kit didn't try to answer. She buried her face in Dad's chest and held on tight. She knew that all her whole life long she would never forget this feeling, this wonderful feeling of being home and safe at last. Then she pulled away from Dad. "I'm so sorry. It's all my fault!" she sputtered. "I wanted an adventure, and I didn't stop to think . . ." She stopped, and swallowed hard. "Will and Stirling are across the river," she said, "in Spencerville. They're . . . they're in jail."

"What?" gasped all the grownups, bewildered. Mrs. Howard held onto Mother as if she were going to faint.

As swiftly as she could, Kit told the whole story. She told how she'd been so stubbornly set on having an adventure that she'd hopped the freight even though Will tried to talk her out of it. She described

56

being rounded up by the railroad bulls and marched to jail. She told how Stirling scribbled the secret sign, and how she escaped, crossed the trestle bridge, and made her way home. Then she turned her dirt-and tear-streaked face to Dad. "We've got to go to Spencerville and rescue Will and Stirling *right now,*" she pleaded. "We've got to get them out of that jail."

Dad nodded. "We'll take Mr. and Mrs. Bell's car," he said. "Come on."

When they got out of the car in Spencerville and walked into the jail, Kit held tightly to Dad's hand. She stood very close, hidden behind him, while he talked to the sheriff about letting Will and Stirling go.

"Go ahead and take these boys," the sheriff said as he released Will and Stirling. "We don't like their sort around here."

Will and Stirling hurried toward Dad with grateful expressions. All three turned toward the door. But Kit held back. She stepped fully into the light so that the sheriff could see her clearly.

"You!" exclaimed the sheriff. "You should be ashamed of yourself!"

Kit looked the sheriff straight in the eyes and spoke in a level voice. "Sir," she said, "I think *you* should be ashamed."

"Hopping freight trains is against the law," said the sheriff. "It's my job to keep bums off trains."

"You don't have to be so mean about it," said Kit. "The hoboes haven't hurt anybody. They're just poor. There's no reason to treat them so badly. It isn't right. And it isn't *fair*."

The sheriff glowered, but he said nothing.

"Come along, Kit," said Dad softly. "It's time to go home."

Kit followed Stirling, Will, and Dad to the car. Stirling climbed into the back seat and Kit sat next to him, leaving room for Will to sit in the front. But Will didn't get into the car.

Kit poked her head out. "Aren't you coming, Will?" she asked.

Will shook his head. "No," he said. "Thanks, but it's time for me to head west to Oregon. I don't want to miss getting a job during the apple harvest."

"Is Montana on your way?" asked Kit.

"I reckon so," said Will. "I'll stop by and say 'hey' to Charlie for you."

Will shook Dad's hand. "Good-bye, sir," he said. "Thanks for everything." Then he smiled his wide, heart-warming grin at Kit and Stirling. "Good-bye, you two," he said.

This time Kit and Stirling could not smile back. "Good-bye, Will," they said. Stirling's voice was low in the darkness, and Kit's voice was sorrowful. She was weighted down with worry, now that she knew how hard Will's life really was. Dad started the car, and Kit knelt on the seat and looked out the back window to wave good-bye to Will. But he had already turned away. He was walking west.

Scrubbed clean, and in their bathrobes, Kit and Stirling sat at the kitchen table. As soon as they'd arrived home, Mother had told them to take baths, then report to the kitchen. Now an unsmiling Aunt Millie poured them tall glasses of cold milk and put plates of hot, buttered toast in front of them.

Mother spoke first. "We are very glad you're

safe, children," she said.

"We were worried sick about you!" exclaimed Mrs. Howard.

"We're sorry," said Kit. "We—"

But Dad held up his hand to stop her. "I understand how it feels to want an adventure," he said. "Sometimes I think the toughest thing about this Depression is enduring it, day after day. But I hope you two understand that what you did was foolish and dangerous. You used poor judgment, and you're lucky you didn't have to pay for it more dearly than you did. I think I speak for Mrs. Howard and Mother and Aunt Millie when I say that we're disappointed in you. We need to trust you to be more sensible in the future. Do you understand?"

Kit and Stirling nodded. They both looked ashamed.

"Well!" said Aunt Millie briskly. "Thank goodness it's all over now. And as Shakespeare says, 'All's well that ends well.'"

Kit managed a weak smile. But as she went up the stairs to her room, with Mother's gentle arm around her, Kit thought that perhaps this time Shakespeare and Aunt Millie were not right. Kit thought of Will and all the hardship that was before him. She thought of the hungry children she'd seen eating the hobo stew. She thought of the poor, tired hoboes gathered around their fire in the jungle, resting their weary, hurt feet. She thought of the hoboes crowded so roughly into the terrible jail. For them, all was not ended and, surely, all was not well.

After Mother kissed her good night, Kit lay awake thinking. *Everyone should see what I saw today,* she thought. *Hoboes have a hard life. People should know that. Someone should tell them. Someone should **do** something. Maybe I could.*

Looking
Back
1934

# A Peek Into
# the Past

*A homeless family
trying to hitch a ride*

In 1934, many Americans were on the move. Some
people started traveling when they lost their jobs and
their homes because of the Depression. They packed all
their belongings into their cars and went in search of new
jobs and new places to settle. Other people, like Kit's
friend Will, hopped onto freight trains and rode in empty
boxcars in search of jobs and adventure. These travelers
were known as *hoboes*. They "rode the rails," or traveled
by train, often with only a bedroll and the clothes they
wore. Hopping freights was illegal and dangerous. Many
people were injured and some even lost their lives doing
it, but most couldn't afford to travel any other way.
Others simply preferred it, thrilling to the adventure of
life on the open road.

*Sitting in a boxcar doorway was dangerous,
even when a train was moving slowly.*

UNION PACIFIC

O. S. L.

300524

During the 1930s, more than 250,000 hoboes rode the rails. Some people were afraid of hoboes and called them *tramps* or *bums*. But to those who lived on the road, there were important differences. As one hobo described it, "A *hobo* is a person who travels to work, a *tramp* is a person who travels and won't work, and a *bum* is a person who won't travel or work." Hoboes often didn't like tramps and bums because of their unwillingness to work, which gave them all a bad reputation.

*Most girls who rode the rails felt safer disguised as boys.*

Most hoboes were men or boys, but girls, women, and even whole families hopped trains to find jobs or to get to another town. When a train pulled into a new town, the hoboes hopped off and started looking for work. If there were no jobs, they sometimes knocked on doors to ask for food in exchange for doing chores. Like Will, most hoboes brought food back to the *jungles*, the hobo camps near rail yards. There, they added it to the large pots of stew that everyone in the jungle shared. Sometimes there was a lot of food and the hoboes ate well, but other times there was barely enough to go around.

*Getting ready for dinner in a hobo jungle*

Even though hoboes helped each other and often found a special sort of community in the jungles, hobo life was harsh and gritty. For many, riding the rails was the only way to find work during the Depression. And while some hoboes spent only a short time on the road, others spent years traveling all around America, even after the end of the Depression.

There were other ways to travel for those who could afford it. People with money could travel by car, train, bus, or even by plane. Air travel was new and still rough in the 1930s—a plane's vibrations could shake a passenger's glasses off his or her nose, and caused airplane seats, which weren't fastened down, to slide about.

*In 1933, First Lady Eleanor Roosevelt (left) flew with pilot Amelia Earhart to show the public that airplane travel was safe.*

*Airline companies used advertisements to reassure passengers of the safety and comfort of airline travel.*

FIRST TIME UP!

Americans who stayed closer to home enjoyed many activities that brought welcome distraction from the Depression. Instead of going away on vacation, as they had before hard times hit, people gathered at home or went to local parks to enjoy family picnics, games and sports, and other outdoor activities.

*Girls found ways to have fun with their friends in spite of the hard times.*

In cities with professional baseball teams, such as Cincinnati, people could forget their troubles for a few hours at a ball game. Miniature golf and drive-in movies also started in the 1930s and quickly grew in popularity.

*Miniature golf was first called "midget golf."*

However, as the Depression got worse, many communities started to run out of money to build and maintain parks and recreation areas—even though the need for free recreation soared. In Racine, Wisconsin, as well as in many other cities, boys had to play baseball in streets or alleys, because park and school baseball diamonds were in constant use by unemployed adult men.

67

*A street baseball game*

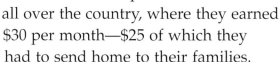

*One of the 1,300 CCC camps set up by June 1933*

The increased need for parks and recreation areas was answered in part by one of the many programs started by President Franklin Roosevelt. Within four weeks of becoming president in March 1933, Roosevelt created the Civilian Conservation Corps, or CCC, which put thousands of men to work building and improving parks, planting trees, digging ditches, improving streams, and fighting fires.

The CCC was made up of young, unmarried men between the ages of 18 and 25. Boys like Kit's brother Charlie were sent to outdoor work camps all over the country, where they earned $30 per month—$25 of which they had to send home to their families. Roosevelt had three goals in sending these young men from the cities to the countryside. He wanted to pro-vide training and employment for

*CCC ditch diggers*

*The government created posters to advertise the CCC.*

68

America's youth, much-needed money for their families at home, and a way to conserve and restore America's natural resources.

Men who enrolled received hats, pins, and booklets describing the CCC.

In the beginning, enrollment in the CCC was limited to six months, but Roosevelt later authorized re-enrollment for those who wanted to remain in the Corps. During the first year, the CCC put 293,000 young men to work. When the program ended in the early 1940s, more than three million men had joined the CCC. It was one of Roosevelt's most popular programs. The next time you go to a state or national park, look for a CCC marker. Think about the young men like Charlie who, through their work for the CCC, improved and protected America's natural areas and gave people like Kit's family hope that America would pull itself out of the Depression.

CCC workers, President Roosevelt (seated, in center), and the men who created the CCC celebrated the signing of papers that authorized re-enrollment in the Corps.

# THE BOOKS ABOUT KIT

### MEET KIT • An American Girl
Kit Kittredge and her family get news that
turns their household upside down.

### KIT LEARNS A LESSON • A School Story
It's Thanksgiving, and Kit learns a surprising
lesson about being thankful.

### KIT'S SURPRISE • A Christmas Story
The Kittredges may lose their house.
Can Kit still find a way to make Christmas
merry and bright for her family?

### HAPPY BIRTHDAY, KIT! • A Springtime Story
Kit loves Aunt Millie's thrifty ideas—until Aunt Millie
plans a pinch-penny party and invites Kit's whole class.

### KIT SAVES THE DAY • A Summer Story
Kit's curiosity and longing for adventure
lead her to unexpected places—and into trouble!

### CHANGES FOR KIT • A Winter Story
Kit writes a letter that brings changes and
new hope—in spite of the hard times.

◆

### WELCOME TO KIT'S WORLD • 1934
American history is lavishly portrayed
with photographs, illustrations, and
excerpts from real girls' letters and diaries.

## MORE TO DISCOVER!

While books are the heart of The American Girls Collection,®
they are only the beginning. The stories in the Collection come
to life when you act them out with the beautiful American Girls
dolls and their exquisite clothes and accessories.
To request a catalogue full of things girls love, you
can send in this postcard, call **1-800-845-0005,**
or visit our Web site at **americangirl.com**.

If the postcard has already been removed from this book and you would like to receive an American Girl® catalogue, please send your name and address to:

*American Girl*
*P.O. Box 620497*
*Middleton, WI 53562-0497*

You may also call our toll-free number, **1-800-845-0005,** or visit our Web site at **americangirl.com**.

Place
Stamp
Here